TOMMY AND TAMMY THE FIREFIGHTING CHILDREN

BOOK #1

"TO THE RESCUE"

BY FIRE FIGHTING CAPTAIN TIM KENNEDY

ILLUSTRATED BY ELIZABETH FERNANDEZ & ERIC DE LA TORRE

To THE EMERGENCY ROOM STAFF!
THANK YOU FOR THE GREAT TREATMENT
YESTERDAY FOR MY BEE STING!
YOU ALL DO GREAT WORK! KEEP IT UP!
I HOPE THESE BOOKS CAN HELP YOUR
CHILD OR A NIECE OR NEPHEW
STAY SAFE!
Capt S Kennedy

This book is dedicated to my daughters
Kayla and Madison, may it help keep children
in the world safe no matter where they live

It all started just like this...

When Tommy's alarm went off, instead of pulling his pillow over his head, letting out a loud moan, and rolling over to fall back to sleep - he sprung out of bed like someone had thrown a bucket of cold water on him!

Today Tammy, his eleven-year-old twin sister, and him had an important test to pass and they were both quite excited!

Tommy walked into the hallway to see
his sister heading toward the bathroom to
take a shower. Tammy was up early and
bubbling with excitement as well!

She looked back over her shoulder and said,
"Are you ready Tommy?"

He quickly replied,
"You bet sister!"

They had been waiting for this day
since last month, when the Mayor had
called a special meeting at city hall.

At that time he had spoken about what
they all should do now that Oyster
Bay's only sawmill had shut down.

People had lined up and filed into the
building. It didn't take long to be filled,
and every last seat was taken.

The last person sat down and everyone anxiously waited for the meeting to start. The Mayor cleared his throat, hit his wooden hammer on the table and said, *"Ahem... ahem … people … people… please do be quiet. As you all know, we have something very important to discuss today."*

The buzz of whispering voices soon died down. There was silence as they leaned forward to hear what the Mayor had to say.

''My good citizens of Oyster Bay... as you know, when the sawmill shut down a lot of people left town to find work elsewhere.''

The people nodded at each other, whispered, and shared their thoughts. The buzz of voices grew louder and once again the Mayor slammed down the wooden hammer to get their attention and to stop talking.

"Now that I have your attention, let me start again... well, good people of Oyster Bay, we have a problem. With so many people leaving our town, we no longer have enough volunteer firefighters."

Once again the townspeople stirred in their seats. The sound of their voices rose even louder. What were they to do?

The Mayor's chubby face was now red and sweaty as he rubbed his hands together. He anxiously looked through his round spectacles at the crowd of worried looking faces, hoping someone would have a solution to their problem.

Tommy and Tammy sat with their parents
and listened to the voices around them. The
twins' father was one of the volunteer firefighters; he was also a fisherman, so he had not
lost his job when the sawmill shut down.

They remembered how they had helped their
father practice tying knots with ropes and putting
ladders up against the side of the house.

Tammy, thinking about all the practice her brother and Tammy had with their father, suddenly had a great idea! Why not have Tommy and me help the town and become volunteer firefighters. They were only eleven, but they certainly had a lot of practice!

Excited, Tammy leaned over and whispered her idea into her father's ear. He sat back in his chair, winked at her, and said, "*Tammy that is an excellent idea my dear.*"

Tommy and Tammy's father proudly stood up
to address the Mayor and the people of their
small town. In his strong voice he suggested,
**"Why not have my twins help us out. They
help me practice firefighting at home all the
time and they're both very good at it."**

He looked very big beside his children and
had the same bright red curly hair and
sparkling light blue eyes they did.

Once again the room buzzed as everyone was speaking at the same time. The
twins loved the idea, but the Mayor would
have to agree with their father.

**As far as they knew there weren't any other
children firefighters anywhere - they would
be the world's first. What a great idea!**

The Mayor brought his small wooden hammer
down hard on to the table once again to hush
the crowd. Again he cleared his voice, *"Ahem,
ahem... okay, my good citizens of Oyster Bay...
I think we need to have a vote to see if this is a
good idea."* The people in the room all nodded in
agreement; this would be the best way to decide.

The Mayor started to pass out small pieces of paper throughout the crowd to write *"yes"* or *"no"* on.

Tammy and Tommy jumped up to help pass the ballots out. They wanted everyone to know they were excited and willing to be firefighters.

Once all of the votes were handed in, the Mayor started to count them one-by-one. The room was quiet as everyone waited for the results.

The twins sat on the edge of their chairs; they leaned forward, eager to find out if they would be able to become the world's youngest firefighters. Their father put his arm around their shoulders to reassure them it would be okay either way.

It seemed to take forever, but the Mayor finally looked up from the pile of small white papers in front of him and said, ***"You have all voted and the twins will have a chance to become volunteer firefighters!"***

Everyone in the room was cheering and had big
smiles on their faces: the biggest smiles were on
the twins' faces. They could not wait to start!

The Mayor spoke again, *"Just one more thing…
the twins will need to train at the fire hall
and pass the Chief's exams and firefighter
drills before they can ride on the fire trucks."*
Tommy and Tammy weren't worried; they
knew their father had taught them well.

Tommy and Tammy trained at the fire hall for weeks. They practiced pulling the fire hose, putting up ladders, and tying all kinds of knots. After training all day they studied the homework Fire Chief Bolton had given them about fire trucks, fire hoses, and first aid in the evenings.

They didn't mind, they both knew it would be worth all the hard work if they passed the test.

Back to this morning...

The weeks of training and learning passed quickly. And today they were going to be tested. They finished getting ready and headed off to the fire hall. They were nervous, but they had worked very hard the last couple of weeks and felt they would do well.

They kept reminding themselves of what their father had told them so many times before, *"If you study and work hard, you can do almost anything you want to do in life!"*

All morning Fire Chief Bolton had them perform
fire and ladder drills. He also had the twins
show him how good they were at giving first aid
and helping rescue people in car accidents.

Later that day, they sat in the fire hall classroom and
wrote the tests he had given them. They needed to
have excellent marks for this part of the test as well.

Finally it was all over and they sat in the hallway outside the Fire Chief's office waiting nervously for him to finish calculating their test results.

They sat in their chairs with their arms around each other. They were a team now and needed to support each other. They clearly understood that firefighting can be dangerous and they needed to work together as a team at all times.

Finally, Fire Chief Bolton came out and with a
huge smile on his face announced, ***"Welcome to
the Oyster Bay Fire Department kids! You both
passed with excellent marks ...well done!"***

They leapt out of their chairs and hugged
each other: it was the best news they
had ever heard in their young lives!

The next day most of the townspeople showed up for their graduation ceremony at the fire hall. They stood at attention in front of the people as Fire Chief Bolton pinned their new, shiny badges on to the front of their new, blue firefighter uniforms.

And there, in the front row, sat their proud parents smiling at their twins. *"Well done Tommy and Tammy! Bravo!"* Both parents held back their tears of joy. **Their very own children were the now world's youngest and first children firefighters!**

TOMMY AND TAMMY'S DO'S AND DON'TS

The Do's

✓ DO test your smoke alarms once a month (or if away for more than 7 days).

✓ DO remind your mom and dad to change your smoke alarm batteries, on clock time changes or birthdays (twice a year minimum).

✓ DO replace your smoke alarms every 10 years (or follow manufacturer's recommendations).

✓ DO install a CO (carbon monoxide) alarm in your house if you use burning appliances (one on each floor, minimum).

✓ DO install smoke alarms on each floor of the house and outside bedrooms (even better, inside bedrooms also, new building and fire codes are moving in this direction)

✓ DO practice a fire drill on your birthday with your mom and dad (even better, twice a year with battery changes in smoke alarms).

✓ DO have a fire safety plan for your home on your bedroom wall.

✓ DO have a rope ladder for your bedroom window if you are high up.

✓ DO yell "Fire! Fire!" to warn others if you smell or hear a fire in your home.

✓ DO tell your mom or dad to cover the pan with a lid if there is a fire on the stove.

✓ DO run ice-cold water over the burn right away for 10–15 minutes if you get burned.

✓ DO close your bedroom door at night and latch it firmly when you go to bed.

---

1   These are general safety recommendations for your family. Please consult your local fire department for their requirements, including local bylaws and fire codes.

The Don'ts

✗ DO NOT ever play with chemicals, electric plugs, gasoline, matches, lighters, or candles.

✗ DO NOT ever go out your bedroom door if it feels hot to touch. Go out the window to the meeting spot marked with the X on the fire safety plan on your bedroom wall.

✗ DO NOT ever hide from a fire. Leave the house right away after yelling "Fire! Fire!"

✗ DO NOT ever stand up in the heat and smoke of a fire. Always stay low.

✗ DO NOT ever put anything that can burn near a heater or a flame.

✗ DO NOT ever go back inside the house once you are safely outside. Leave the rescue of pets to the firefighters.

✗ DO NOT ever play with fire. If your clothes catch on fire, drop to the ground and roll until the flames are out. If you see a person doing this, you can help by putting your coat on them to help smother the fire.

✗ DO NOT ever leave pot handles turned outward on the stove.

✗ DO NOT ever throw cigarettes out of car windows.

✗ DO NOT leave a burning campfire. Always pull the wood apart and pour water on the fire until it is cool to touch.

Spot the DANGER!

Fire Drill Procedures

- When you hear the smoke alarm, go to your door and touch it with the back of your hand, starting at the bottom. Move your hand from the bottom up the door to see if it is hot (do not touch the metal handle on the door).

- If it is not hot, open the door slowly and be ready to close it if smoke rushes into your bedroom. If it is OK, follow your smoke-free exit route. Quickly make your way to the family meeting spot outside. (Yell "Fire! Fire!" to warn others inside as you leave.)

- If the door is hot, or if smoke rushes in, go to your window and use that exit to reach the family meeting area.

- **Hints**

- It's a good idea to keep a flashlight and a whistle by the window for signaling fire-fighters if you can't exit on your own.

- It's a good idea to test smoke alarms with fire drills so children associate the sound with fire and wake up. (Many kids can sleep through the sound of smoke alarms.)

Tommy and Tammy Fire Safety Plan

(SEE INSTRUCTIONS ON NEXT PAGE)

NAME: _____'s bedroom

(PRINT A COPY FOR EACH CHILD'S BEDROOM)

Tommy and Tammy Fire Safety Plan Instructions

1- Draw home's floor plan

2- Mark in at least two ways out to family meeting spot

3- Draw and X at family meeting spot

4- Talk about what to do in a fire with children on their birthdays:

. check door for heat, starting at the bottom
. do not touch metal knob
. If the door is NOT HOT
  open the door a little, look out to see if it's ok
. If the hallway is full of heavy smoke
  close the door tightly and use the window

Example:

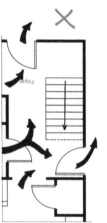

The 'X' marks the meeting spot

Tommy and Tammy Fire Safety Plan

NAME: _____'s bedroom

(SEE INSTRUCTIONS FOR REFERENCE)

Tommy and Tammy Fire Safety Plan Instructions

1- Draw home's floor plan

2- Mark in at least two ways out to family meeting spot

3- Draw and X at family meeting spot

4- Talk about what to do in a fire with children on their birthdays:

. check door for heat, starting at the bottom
. do not touch metal knob
. If the door is NOT HOT
   open the door a little, look out to see if it's ok
. If the hallway is full of heavy smoke
   close the door tightly and use the window

Example:

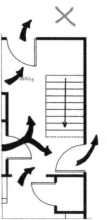

The 'X' marks the meeting spot

Tommy and Tammy Fire Safety Plan

(SEE INSTRUCTIONS FOR REFERENCE)

NAME: _____'s bedroom

(PRINT A COPY FOR EACH CHILD'S BEDROOM)

Tommy and Tammy Fire Safety Plan Instructions

1- Draw home's floor plan

2- Mark in at least two ways out to family meeting spot

3- Draw and X at family meeting spot

4- Talk about what to do in a fire with children on their birthdays:

. check door for heat, starting at the bottom

. do not touch metal knob

. If the door is NOT HOT
  open the door a little, look out to see if it's ok

. If the hallway is full of heavy smoke
  close the door tightly and use the window

Example:

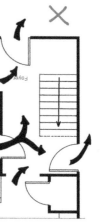

The 'X' marks the meeting spot

*Tommy and Tammy's adventures
will continue in*

Tommy and Tammy
The Firefighting Children
"Their First Fire"

Acknowledgements

I want to thank my wife Jane for her backing me in the writing of this story to help keep children safe wherever they maybe in the world. I would also like to thank my friend Monique Bois for her helping me with the editing of the book.

A special thanks to my illustrators Elizabeth and Eric for all their hard work in helping me make my story of the world's only firefighting children come to life.

Lastly but not least …a special thank you to all of you parents out there that support my book and put up the fire safety plans on your children's bedroom walls showing at least two routes out to the safe meeting area and discuss your family fire safety plan with your children on their birthdays to help ensure they have many more.

Thank You All,
Captain Tim Kennedy

These Books Are Available At:

OUR WEBSITE
firefightingchildren.com
email us for best pricing
firefightingchildren@hotmail.com

OR

All online book sites
FriesenPress Bookstore
Save-On-Food Stores

Thank you for your efforts
to help keep children safer!

 FriesenPress

Suite 300 - 990 Fort St
Victoria, BC, Canada, V8V 3K2
www.friesenpress.com

Contact the author at firefightingchildren@hotmail.com

ISBN
978-1-4602-6790-5 (Paperback)
978-1-4602-6791-2 (eBook)

1. Juvenile Fiction, Action & Adventure

Distributed to the trade by The Ingram Book Company

CPSIA information can be obtained
at www.ICGtesting.com
Printed in the USA
LVHW070741280519
619218LV00002B/8/P